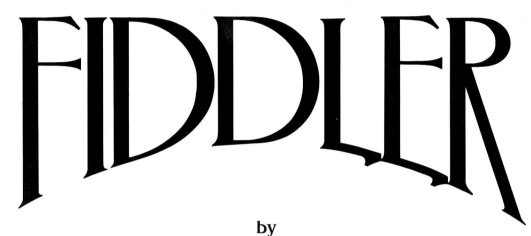

FIDDLER

by
Stephen Cosgrove
Illustrated by
Wendy Edelson

MULTNOMAH · PRESS
10209 SE Division Street, Portland, Oregon 97266

Library of Congress Cataloging-in Publication Data

Cosgrove, Stephen.
   Fiddler / written by Stephen Edward Cosgrove ;
illustrated by Wendy Edelson.

   Summary: The bears in Barely There live shut up in
their houses, each refusing to share his own special
food with the others, until a strange new bear comes
along with some new ideas.
   [1. Sharing—Fiction.   2. Bears—Fiction]
I. Edelson, Wendy, ill.   II. Title.
PZ7. C8187Fi   1987   [Fic]   87-20989
ISBN 0-88070-235-4

Dedicated to the Grames Gang
(Darell Sr., Darell Jr., Darell III, Teresa,
Tyler, Cindy, Sandie, Scott, Shaerie,
Shannon, Grandma and Grandpa).
A great group but a gang just the same.
Stephen

"Do unto others
as you would have them
do unto you."
—according to the Gospels

nce upon a time and farther than far at the very edge of the horizon was a path bordered with lacy fern. If you walked down that path following the dancing squirrels and singing birds you would find a land called *Barely There*.

Barely There . . . a land filled with
magic . . . a land where the wind
whispers through the giant pines
then suddenly whips a crinkled,
orange leaf high into the sky to float
in lazy circles back to the forest floor
and the land called *Barely There*.

Down the fern-bordered path was a quiet, shadowy glade. In the glade beside the path were short, squatty cabins made of pitch, pine, and poplar. In the cabins with shutters drawn lived the bears of *Barely There*. It didn't look as if bears lived there . . . it didn't look as if any bears were home.

But if you looked very carefully you could see wisps of smoke sneakily slip from the chimneys of riverstone rock. Look again! Here and there behind shutters barred and doors locked tight lived and hid the bears of *Barely There*. For you see, the bears didn't trust anybody, not even themselves.

All the cabins would have stayed quietly boarded up and secreted away; all the bears would have stayed hidden from each other but for the day there came music to the land of *Barely There* in the shape of a whistling bear.

This bear didn't sneak from pine to pine like the other bears. This bear danced down the middle of the path of lacy ferns as he whistled a tune. Beneath his arm he carried a mysterious, odd-shaped package that seemed like nothing more than wrapped bumps and lumps.

He nearly walked by the little cabins in the woods, but then he stopped! He looked at the cabins, smiled a great big smile, and stepped off the path. He walked right up to the first cabin and knocked musically on the door not once, not twice, but thrice. Rap! Rap! Rap!

There came from the cabin the flopping noise of furry slippers on worn wooden floors. With a creak the door opened a crack, and two large eyes peeked out at this whistling bear. The eyes looked and then looked again as the door opened a bit wider. "Uhh, what do you want?" asked a fuzzy voice.

The whistling bear didn't talk like you and me; he sang whatever he said.

"My name is Fiddler, and you see I come from the land of Frippery. I have walked here with a rhythm and a beat. May I come in and rest my feet?

Then, with a smile and a short bow, he walked right into the cabin without so much as, "Excuse me!" or "By your leave!"

Fiddler plopped himself down in a big old chair right beside the table of plain pine planks. He placed his oddly wrapped package on the table before him and drummed his fingers in time.

"Uhh, my name is E. Azalea Bear," she said as her paw went nervously from mouth to cheek to apron. "I don't rightly remember what the E. stands for."

Fiddler laughed and sang, *"I like your name but I don't care. Have you some food you'd like to share?"*

E. Azalea looked at him suspiciously
and said, "Mister Fiddler Bear, I am known
far and wide for my barley bran biscuits. *But
. . .* I am not giving them away for free!"

Fiddler smiled a secret smile then sang
this simple song, *"Your biscuits are great,
this I've been told, and for them I'll trade
more value than gold!"*

"More value than gold? Hmmm!" she
said. "You'll have your biscuits Mister
Fiddler Bear!"

She ground up some barley and bran into coarse flour. She mixed, whisked, and whipped that flour into a batter that was better than any other. As the biscuits bubbled and baked, she danced about the cabin, her skirts skittering on the floor while Fiddler hummed an old bear tune. When the biscuits were baked, Fiddler ate them all, even the crumbs! He then leaned back in the chair and sang, *"Those biscuits were fine, they tasted just great! But something is missing in what I just ate!"*

E. Azalea paced about muttering and mumbling, "I know! I know! Bumbleberries are what's missing! That miserly old Francis T. Bear from right next door won't give me any bumbleberies to make my biscuits better. I just don't trust that old geezer! If I asked for bumbleberries he'd want biscuits!" *"Well, well, well,"* sang Fiddler with a smile. *"I'll slip next door and talk to Francis for a while!"*

With E. Azalea peeking through her shutters, Fiddler danced next door carrying his odd-shaped package. Like no one before, he pounded on the door of Francis T. Bear's house. After much creaking and cracking the door finally opened and there stood a very confused bear dressed only in red long underwear. "Uhh, may I help you?" he asked.

"My name is Fiddler, and you see I come from the land of Frippery. Hungry I am. Hungry I'm very. May I have some of your bumbleberries?"

Old Francis T. was a bit flustered but answered, "Yes, but I just don't give them away!"

Fiddler smiled a secret smile then sang this simple song, *"Your berries are great, this I've been told, and for them I'll trade more value than gold!"*

"More value than gold? Hmmm!" he said. "You'll have your berries Mister Fiddler Bear!" With that the two of them went inside and closed the door.

Fiddler put his package on the table and sat down in the rocking chair made of oiled hickory and oak. He rocked back and forth with a rhythm and a beat.

Francis T. was as nervous as could be for no one had ever been to his cabin before. He blustered about and found a burl bowl of polished pine. He filled it to the brim with bumbleberries all plump and purple and plopped it down in front of Fiddler without even a spoon or napkin.

Fiddler tasted one and then tasted two. He smiled and sang, *"Those berries were fine, they tasted just great! But something is missing in what I just ate!"*

"I know! I know what's missing!" said a frantic Francis T. Bear. "Honey from the butterbees. But that old Emily Z. who lives right next door won't give me any. I don't trust that crotchety bear. She probably would want some of my bumbleberries in return!

"Well, well, well," sang Fiddler with a smile. *"I'll slip next door and talk to Emily awhile!"*

Fiddler, with his odd-shaped package under his arm, skipped down the path and up on the cabin porch of Emily Z. Bear. He knocked and he knocked. Rap-a-tap-tap. Rap-a-tap-tap.

There was a long pause. Finally Emily Z. cracked open her door. "Uhhh, may I help you, young bear?"

"You surely may, ma'am!" sang Fiddler with a smile. *"My name is Fiddler, and you see I come from the land of Frippery. Hungry I am and I don't have money. May I please have just a taste of your honey?"*

"No money, huh!" she said with a growl. "Then why should I give you a taste of my honey?"

Fiddler smiled a secret smile then sang this simple song, *"Your honey is great, this I've been told. For a taste I'll trade more value than gold!"*

"More value than gold you say. Well, come inside Mr. Fiddler Bear, you shall have a taste." With that the two of them went inside.

Emily Z. rustled about and found an old wooden spoon. She slowly dipped it into a big wooden cask that sat on a stool. Her wrists twisted and twirled as she drew up the honey golden as the sun and thicker than taffy. Patting her hair behind her ear, she passed the spoon to Fiddler who took a long slurping taste.

He smiled a secret smile and then sang, *"That honey was fine, it tasted just great! But something is missing in what I just ate!"*

"I know…I know…I know," mumbled Emily Z. as she paced back and forth with her hands clasped behind her. "Biscuits and berries would taste great with my honey, but those neighbors of mine won't give me any. I just don't trust those miserly bears. They'd just want honey in return, and I'll be jiggered if I'll give it to them!"

"Hmmm," hummed Fiddler as he drummed his claws clickity-click on the table top. Then without saying a simple "How do you do!" he grabbed his odd-shaped package and walked out the door.

With three sets of eyes watching from three wooden cabins, Fiddler picked up branches and sticks from the forest floor. He stacked the wood neatly to the side of the path of lacy fern. Then, with a click of flint, he lit a fire and it began to glow.

For the first time in a long time that forest glade warmed as the smoke curled gently about the boughs and branches of the trees. When the fire was crackling and snapping nicely, he sat with a thump on an overturned stump and began to unwrap the odd-shaped package that he had carried wherever he went.

Fold by fold, Fiddler unwrapped the package until the golden light of the roaring fire revealed a finely polished fiddle of bonewood, with strings like the silvered strands of a spiderweb drenched in morning dew. Carefully, he took from the package a long, narrow bow. He placed the fiddle under his chin and began passing the bow softly across the strings.

The music seeped like fog throughout the forests of this land call *Barely There*. The melodies, soft and sweet, quieted even the noisy birds as they perched in the trees. Music, mysterious, melodious music, soothed and warmed the glade of lacy fern and pine.

One by one the doors of the cabins opened wider and wider until each of the bears, from E. Azalea to Emily Z., stood unabashedly listening to the haunting music played by Fiddler.

The music was so beautiful that it seemed to be on loan . . . never meant to be owned. The bears came haltingly out of their seclusion, each carrying a bit of those secret foods they had hoarded for years. E. Azalea with her barley bran biscuits, Francis T. with his purple bumbleberries, and Emily Z. with a crock full of butterbee honey.

As the music danced upon the flames of the fire, the bears offered their gifts to Fiddler who stopped his fiddle playing and softly sang, *"The payment I give, the payment I owed, is as I said more valued than gold. It's not the music, the music I give, but the gift of sharing is the way to live. Now, share all your biscuits, berries, and honey, you'll find sharing love is better than money."*

With that he tuned up his fiddle, rosined up his bow, and with a tap of his foot he let it all go.

Other books
in this series

Shadow Chaser
Gossamer
Derby Downs